There Really is a Santa Claus

The True Story

Written by Cheryl Kvalvik

Illustrated by Lydia Bullock

There Really is a Santa Claus

The True Story

ISBN | 979-8-9913976-1-2

Illustrations by Lydia Bullock

This book is dedicated to all the children of the world, because you are loved.

In the Far North, more North than the North Pole, there is a giant workshop with millions of helpers.

These helpers are not making toys like we would call toys, they have a much more important job to do.

They work for the master builder.

Their job is to help him build a new kingdom and to watch out for children.

All children are invited to
come live in this kingdom.

He does see you when you are sleeping
and when you are awake.

He knows what you love
and what you think.

He is full of goodness and kindness.

He loves you!

He does have good and perfect gifts
for everyone, but because some children
do not want them, they miss out.
His gifts live inside of us to make us
better and much happier.

He never sleeps or takes vacations.
You don't need to write him letters
because he listens every time you talk to Him!

He doesn't need a sleigh because
He rides on clouds, and sometimes on horses.

He doesn't go down chimneys because
He can go through walls.

His hair is like wool and
His eyes twinkle with fire.

His shoes are shiny and bright and
His robe is white with red trim on the bottom.

For those who choose to be on His List, He allows them to come and live with Him in His land, when it is the right time, that is.

Do you want to be on His list?

Just believe in Him and ask Him into your heart.

Then sign your name!

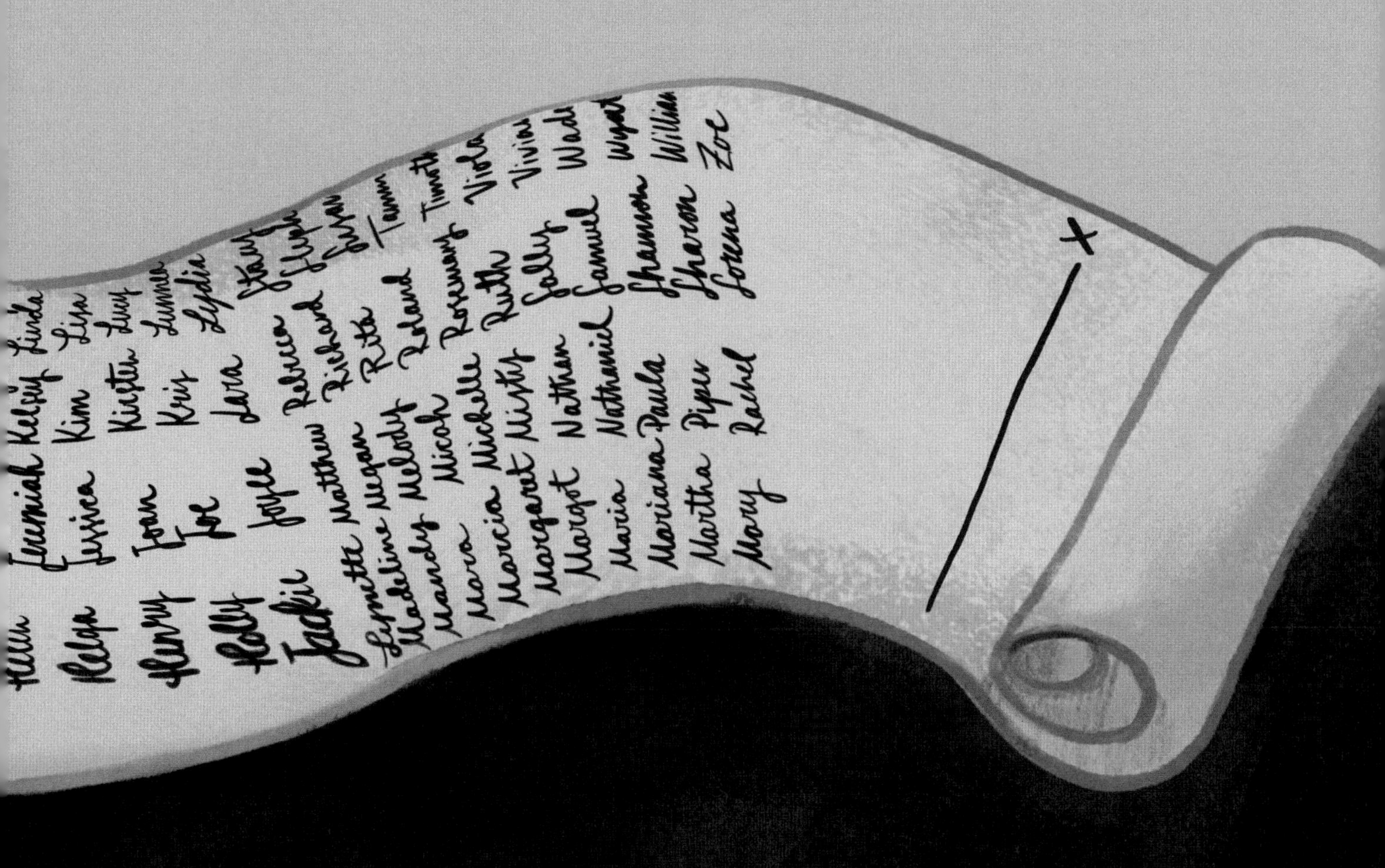

The best gift He has given is Himself.
He gave His life for anyone who wants to be forgiven.

He lived, died, and rose from the dead-
then went back to His wonderful Northern Kingdom.

You see, He is invincible!

He likes toys and candy, but more than that,
He wants His Spirit to be inside of us all the time.

Then the joy of Christmas is with us forever!

Christmas is when we celebrate the time he spent on Earth.

It is a good time to sing "Happy Birthday" to Him and ask him to be with us all year long.

He will remove all the dirty coal from our hearts.

He will forgive us if we ask him to!

His name isn't Santa Claus, which is a nice name,
but His name is:

Jesus Christ, The Bright and Morning Star,
The Light of the World,
The One Who Cares for Me.

He isn't magical but miraculous.

He has all the power needed to make us,
and then, to make us happy.

He knows everything, even our deepest thoughts.
He cares for everyone, rich and poor,
small and great, old and young.

We can't see Him, but we can see what He does.

Made in the USA
Middletown, DE
02 January 2025